STORY BY Mick Szydlowski & Travis Bossard
ILLUSTRATED BY Alex Novoseltsev

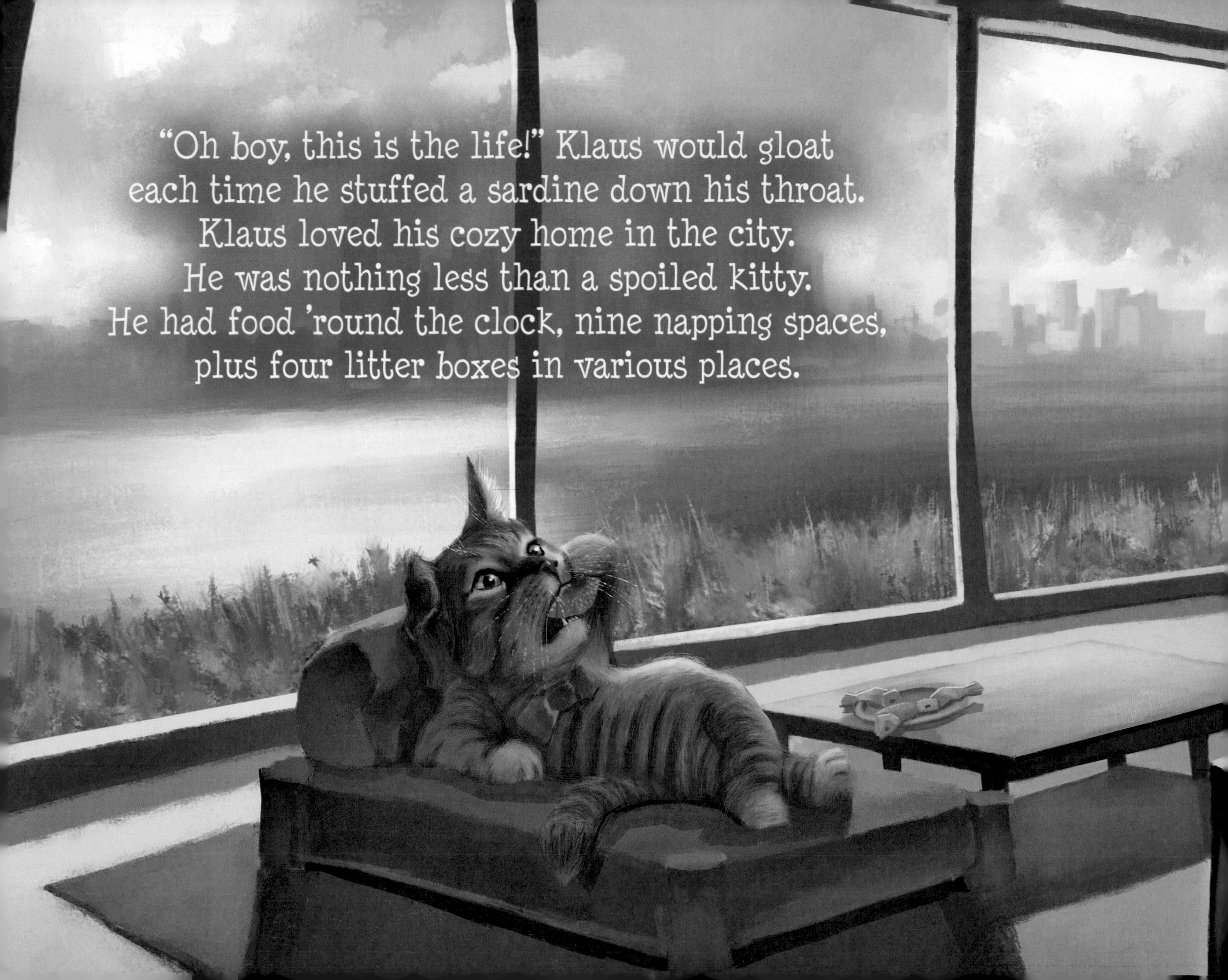

"Oh boy, this is the life!" Klaus would gloat
each time he stuffed a sardine down his throat.
Klaus loved his cozy home in the city.
He was nothing less than a spoiled kitty.
He had food 'round the clock, nine napping spaces,
plus four litter boxes in various places.

"Don't eat too much!" Oskar warned as he climbed.
"Being sick far from home is not a good time."
Then reaching the perch six feet off the floor
he climbed back down and did it once more.
"Tomorrow's the big day, and we must feel good;
we're going camping in Mossy Wood!"

R3B 3L5
MossyWood National Forest
U.S. DEPARTMENT OF AGRICULTURE
US

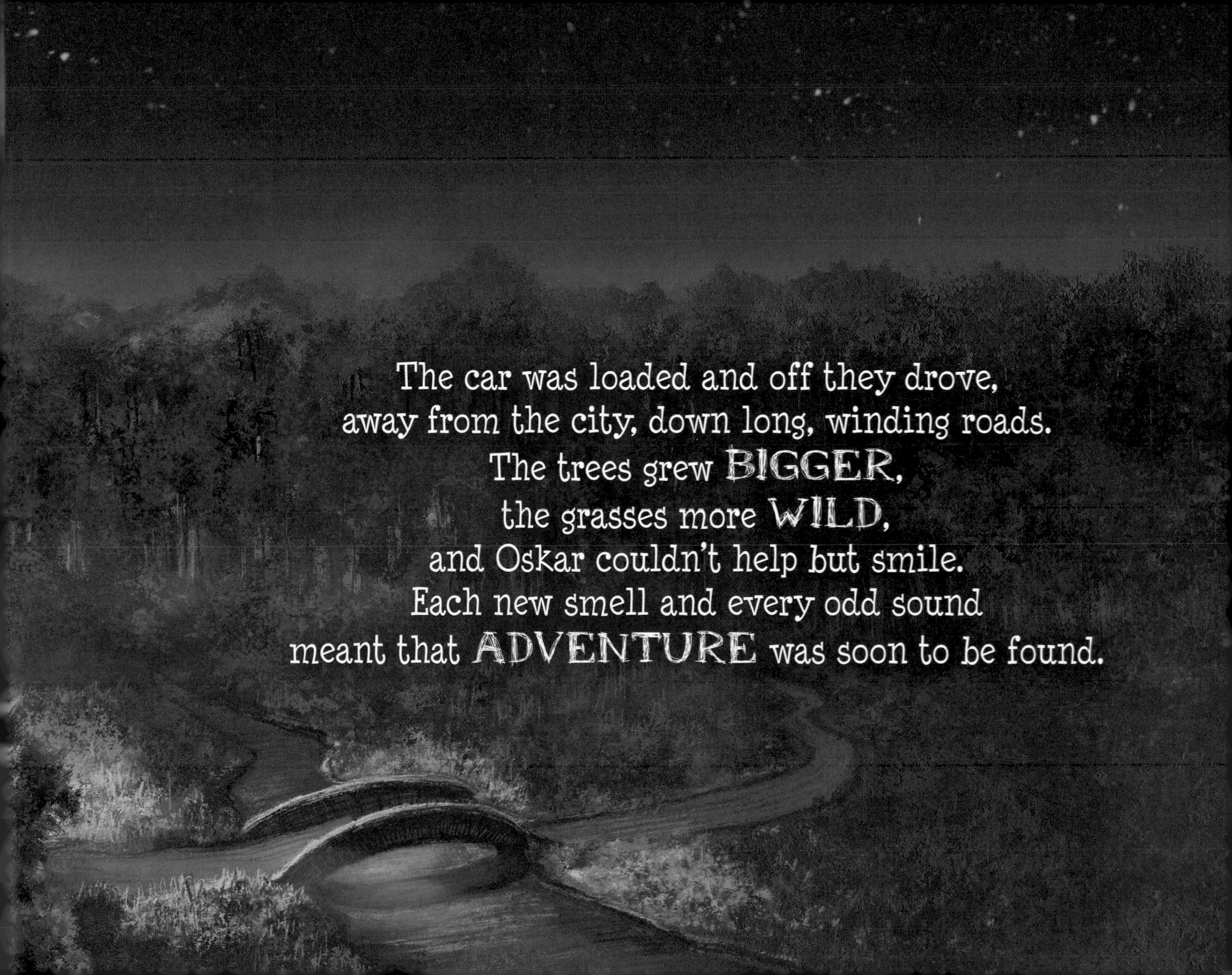

The car was loaded and off they drove,
away from the city, down long, winding roads.
The trees grew BIGGER,
the grasses more WILD,
and Oskar couldn't help but smile.
Each new smell and every odd sound
meant that ADVENTURE was soon to be found.

The tents were pitched by the crackling fire
as shadows danced higher and higher.
They heard the legend of Bigfoot that night
and it gave Klaus a most awful fright!

"When nighttime falls, he steps from his lair
on two HUGE feet, each covered with HAIR.
Like a grizzly bear, he stands TALL and MEAN—
but sly, old Bigfoot is RARELY SEEN.

And all who seek this FEARSOME CREATURE
will never, EVER forget their adventure."

Oskar could not fall asleep in his tent,
"I can find Bigfoot, just by his scent!
Hey, Klaus … Klaus, are you awake?"
"I'm sleeping … " Klaus mumbled, "for goodness sake."
"You are coming with me!" Oskar insisted.
"You have no choice!" He was very persistent.

Klaus rolled over and covered his head
but Oskar pulled him straight from the bed,
out of the tent, and onto the grass.
"Let's get moving! Adventure at last!"

They walked for a while—sometimes they'd jog—
until they reached an old hollow log.
In that spot, the path simply ended.
"Let's go back to the camp!" Klaus demanded.

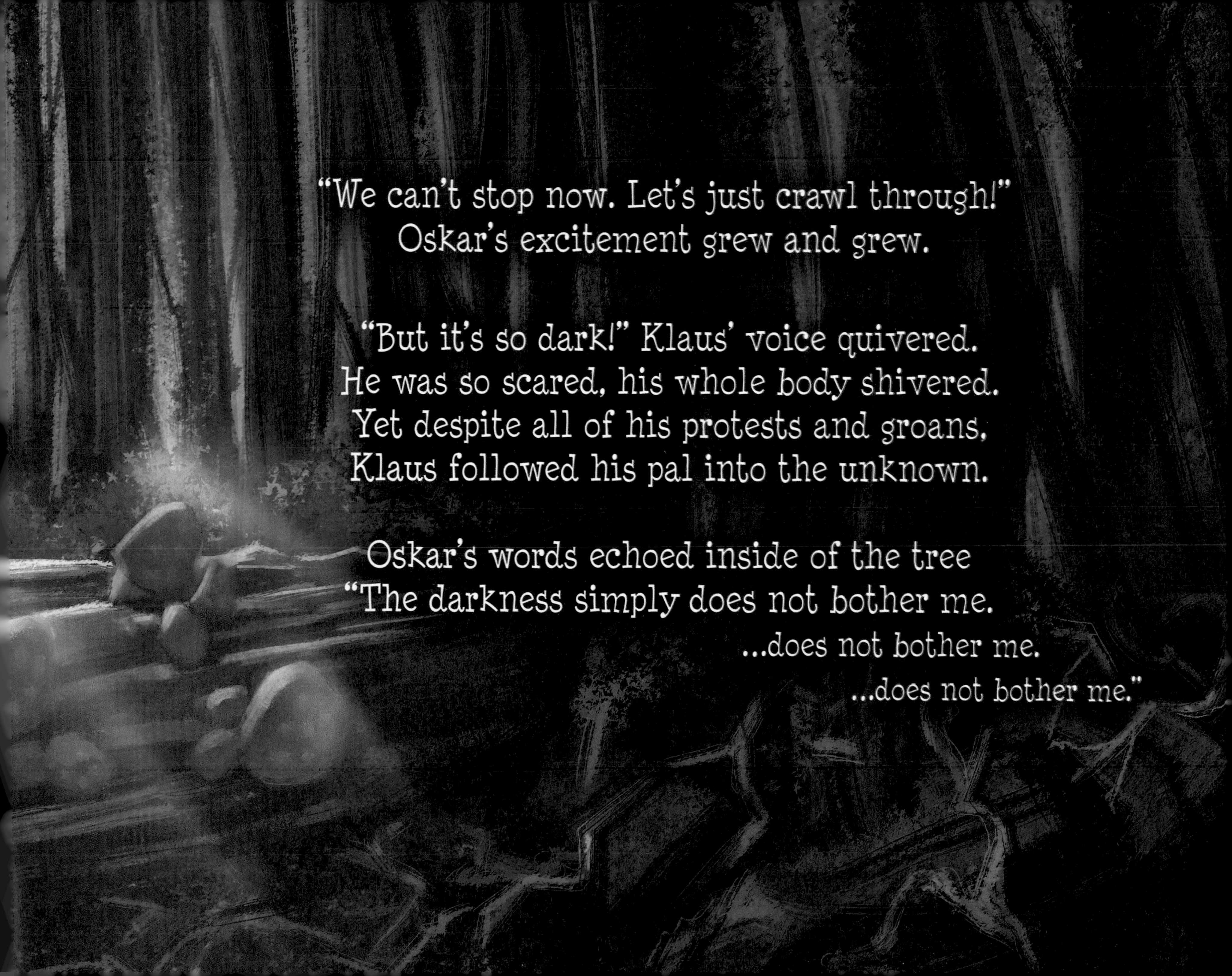

"We can't stop now. Let's just crawl through!"
Oskar's excitement grew and grew.

"But it's so dark!" Klaus' voice quivered.
He was so scared, his whole body shivered.
Yet despite all of his protests and groans,
Klaus followed his pal into the unknown.

Oskar's words echoed inside of the tree
"The darkness simply does not bother me.
...does not bother me.
...does not bother me."

On the other side, they found rushing water,
and swimming on top, a curious otter.
"Hello!" Oskar yelled, "Will you help us across?"
The otter swam closer and said, "Sure thing, boss!"

"Just hop on my back and be sure to hang on.
The stream isn't wide, but the current is strong."
"No, thank you!" cried Klaus, "I can do it **MY** way;
I was swim team co-captain back in the day."

"Now I remember why I quit the team!"
A wet Klaus shivered in a silver moon beam.

Perched high on a branch, sat a serious owl,
her big eyes squinting, beak bent in a scowl.
She asked, "Where is it that you all are headed?"
"To find Bigfoot!" Oskar leapt as he said it.

The owl screeched,
"I heard he's a **BRUTE**!
Is he even **REAL**?!
I don't give a **HOOT**!"

Oskar replied, "Why not join our quest?
It could be good for you
to come out of your nest."
The owl agreed and fluffed her gray feathers,
and the four made a pact to stick close together.

The owl flew high to find a clear path;
the others ran—Klaus was soon out of breath.
A murky haze closed in from each side,
and Oskar's nose was their only guide.

Winding through trees and over old logs,
they kept moving deeper in spite of the fog.
Klaus cried out from the back with a fuss,
"It feels like something is following us!"

Then they heard a SNAP!
Followed by a RUSTLE!

Oskar paused. "I sense something near!"
A mysterious figure began to appear.

"Who goes there?" the nervous otter said.
The puzzled owl just scratched her head.

Klaus proclaimed, "It must be a bug!"

"Actually, I'm a banana slug!"

the stranger explained and then added more.

"For quite some time I've watched you four.

You're all clearly lost and walking in circles.

I'm happy to help, though I'm slow as a turtle.

I know all the shortcuts, so come right along.

To Bigfoot's house! Let's sing a song!"

As the fog grew THICKER and THICKER, the new friends sang to help stick together.

"We STOMP our paws—we SHAKE our tails.
To Bigfoot's house—we make the trail.

Right then left—right, left, right.
We laugh and sing—and march all night.

There's room for all—fast or slow.
We make the trail—as we go!

Right then left—right, left, right.
Through foggy woods—we march all night."

When they finished singing the final chorus,
strange sounds filled the nighttime forest.
Crickets chirped. Frogs croaked.
"This must be the spot!" the banana slug spoke.

That's when Klaus **REALLY** lost his cool.
"What have I done? I've been such a fool
to believe that Bigfoot could truly exist—
and now we're lost in this forest mist!

I wish I was back at our warm, safe camp
with my sleeping bag and handy lamp
and the yummy snacks that I love so much—
and human hands—I miss their touch.

The worst part: **NO ONE IS PETTING ME!**"

Klaus rubbed up on a **BIG** ... hairy ... tree ...

AAAHH ... AAAAHHH ...

ACHOOOOOO!

A sneeze **THUNDERED** forth
from a **HUGE** mouth and nose!
BIGFOOT cleared the fog! The five friends just froze.

"Pardon me," Bigfoot sniffled. He felt kind of silly.
"I'm allergic to cats," he said, picking a lily.
His soothing, kind voice put the whole gang at ease
as the smell of baked goodies blew in on the breeze.

"Won't you all join me in my humble home?
No one ever visits. I'm always alone.
Just follow me; it's not far at all.
I live right behind that blue waterfall."

The home was filled with all sorts of treasure,
which Bigfoot displayed with great care and pleasure:

framed pictures, glass bottles,
an old cookie tin,
jazz record collection,
and recycling bin.

GROWL!

Klaus' belly made the old owl jump back.

Bigfoot chimed in,
"Shall we have a small snack?"

"Try my seasoned pine nuts, gooseberry popovers,
and mushroom sliders garnished with clovers.
Or crabapple scones with raccoon milk brie!
You wouldn't believe, but it's all gluten-free!

And the whistling kettle you hear and see—
is filled with delicious nettle tea!"

They ate by the bushel.
They drank by the gallon.
All were amazed by Bigfoot's talent.

He was HAIRY, TALL, and RARE, indeed,
and ... a GENEROUS soul, they all agreed.

The new friends were laughing.
They abandoned all care.
Klaus stepped outside for a breath of fresh air.
The birds were CHIRP-ing.
The bees were BUZZ-ing.
The breeze was so warm and the fog was gone.
That's when Klaus noticed the sun.

The SUN? THE SUN?!
"THE SUN IS UP!" Klaus shouted with panic.

"We have to get back or we'll never get home!
PLEASE HELP US, BIGFOOT!
WE CAN'T MAKE IT ALONE!"

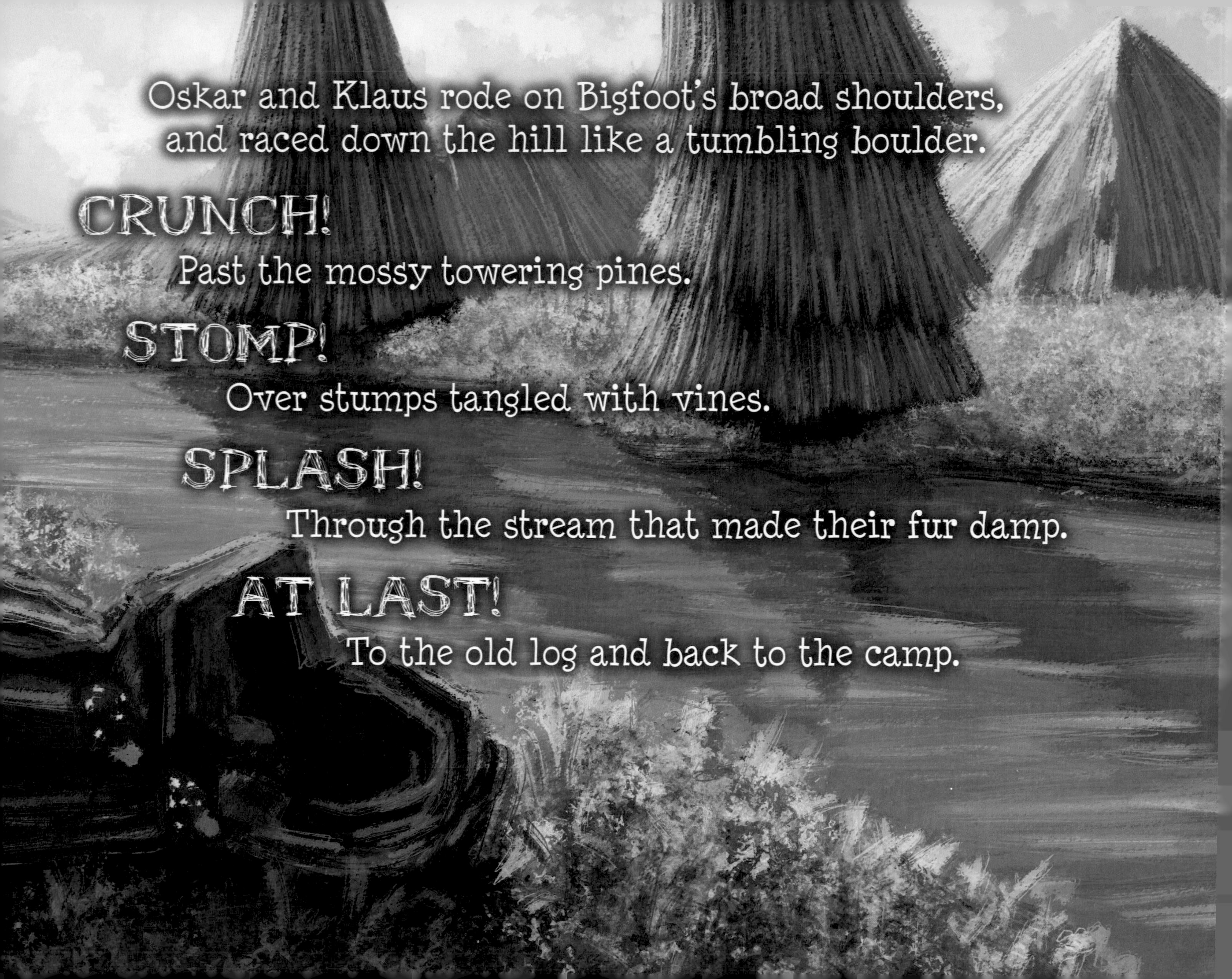

Oskar and Klaus rode on Bigfoot's broad shoulders,
and raced down the hill like a tumbling boulder.

CRUNCH!

Past the mossy towering pines.

STOMP!

Over stumps tangled with vines.

SPLASH!

Through the stream that made their fur damp.

AT LAST!

To the old log and back to the camp.

"It feels like we're flying!" Oskar declared,
but Klaus just held on, a little bit scared.

"Hooray! We made it, and just by a whisker!"
said Oskar to Klaus and Klaus to Oskar.

But just as they dozed off in their cozy, warm bed,
they heard a commotion and a stern voice said:

"It's time to head home, and you two are still snoring?!"
He was unaware of their nighttime exploring.
"And why are you covered in all of that crud?
Your fur is a mess—paws crusty with mud!"
Oskar nudged Klaus and it made them both giggle.
They were laughing so hard, they started to wiggle.

Oskar and Klaus left with wild memories
of searching for Bigfoot among mossy trees
with their new forest friends who helped them along,
and the joy that they shared in singing a song.
From the dread of being lost in the foggy woods,
to the delight of Bigfoot's delicious baked goods!

Now Klaus can finally return to his leisure
while Oskar dreams of their
NEXT BIG ADVENTURE!

This book would not have been possible without the generous support of our Kickstarter backers; thank you for helping to bring this project to life!

We would like to give special thanks to Cecilia Badanes & Weather Enos, Brian & Monica Bossard, Mike & Sherri Bossard, Julie Catron, John & Sherry Douceur, Sally & Randy Knight and Their Feline Family, Rebecca Knox, John Lukas + Max & Shoogie, Debbe McCall, Gail Noblot, Kathy Novakovic, and June Samadi & Brandon Holmes.

We dedicate this book to adventurers everywhere: young or old, big or small!

For information, contact: Oskar & Klaus Inc., P.O. Box 99344, Seattle, WA 98139.

Printed in the United States of America

First Edition - October 2014

ISBN: 978-0-9907843-0-2

Additional information can be found at www.OSKARandKLAUS.com